J. J. Grandville,   Florian

The Fables of Florian

J. J. Grandville, Florian

The Fables of Florian

ISBN/EAN: 9783744778985

Printed in Europe, USA, Canada, Australia, Japan

Cover: Foto ©Andreas Hilbeck / pixelio.de

More available books at **www.hansebooks.com**

THE FABLES

OF

FLORIAN

Fully Illustrated by

J. J. GRANDVILLE.

TRANSLATED FROM THE FRENCH BY

GEN. J. W. PHELPS,

LATE MEMBER OF THE VERMONT HISTORICAL SOCIETY, AUTHOR OF
"A HISTORY OF MADAGASCAR," ETC.

NEW YORK:
JOHN B. ALDEN, PUBLISHER.
1888.

TABLE OF CONTENTS.

TABLE OF CONTENTS.

PREFACE.

JEAN PIERRE CLARIS DE FLORIAN, the author from whose fables the following selections have been made, was born in 1755, in the Chateau de Florian, at the foot of the Cevennes in Languedoc, France. His mother was a lady of beauty and excellence of character, of Spanish origin, whose maiden name was Gilette de Salgué. One of his uncles had married a niece of Voltaire, and it was probably through Voltaire's influence that at the age of thirteen he became a page in the family of the Duke de Penthièvre, a nobleman of great worth and distinction, who was respected even by his enemies.

From the house of this nobleman Florian went to Ferney to complete his education. It was there, while imbibing a taste for letters, that he excited a lively interest in Voltaire, who was pleased by his frank, talented, and amiable conversation, and used occasionally to help him in getting his lessons. It is creditable to the independence and integrity of Florian's character that, although brought at an early age under the influence of a genius so winning and powerful as that of Voltaire, he yet preserved his individuality and followed a literary career peculiarly his own, which was quite opposite to that of his old and gifted friend.

At the age of sixteen Florian entered the artillery school of Bapaume. It appears that he was very well pleased with the military profession, and from the royal corps of artillery he joined, as Lieutenant, the Dragoon regiment of Penthièvre, where he was promoted to a Captaincy. But as he advanced in years, his attach-

6   *FLORIAN'S FABLES.*

ment to letters seems to have acquired the ascendency over his military tastes. He became a prolific and popular writer; but among all his works probably his Fables will longest retain a hold of public appreciation. They have been translated into many languages, and have run through more than one hundred editions.

Though he had exercised the office of gentleman-in-ordinary and almoner to the Duke de Penthièvre, and had in that capacity administered relief to the poor with great delicacy and benevolence, yet when the revolution broke out he was accused of writing verses in honor of the queen, and hurried off to prison. He lived for a time in momentary expectation of death; for his prison, that of La Bourbe, had come to be noted as the inevitable first step towards the scaffold. The death of Robespierre, however, restored him to liberty; but his imprisonment seemed to have left a melancholy shade upon his spirit that time never fully removed. He died on the 17th of September, 1794, in the thirty-ninth year of his age.

There is perhaps no especial value in the present translation over those which may have gone before it; but its interest is heightened by preserving the illustrations of J. J. Grandville, which are fine specimens of French art as it existed some half a century ago. While they are hardly inferior to the best of such productions of the present day, from any school of art, it is believed that they will prove to be highly entertaining to the reader. It must be admitted that the artist has done his author full justice, although the fables are so highly esteemed by some that they have been favorably compared with, and even equalled, to those of La Fontaine. The world will hardly assent to that opinion, perhaps, but still Florian's fables will ever be found interesting and instructive, and for this reason these selections from them are now offered to the American public.

FLORIAN'S FABLES.

TRUTH AND FABLE.

At length among mankind to dwell,
Truth came, all naked, from her well.
By living there so long alone,
She had a little passée grown:
And old and young all fled surpris'd
The moment she was recogniz'd.
Poor Truth remain'd confounded quite
By such an unsuspected slight.
    Just then she chanc'd to see
    Fable in all her finery,
Trick'd out in plumes and diamonds, too

(The most of these were false, 'tis true,
But yet were dazzling to the view),
Who, in familiar courtesy,
Exclaimed: "Oh, here you are, I see!
And quite alone, too, I observe.
            Why are you here,
                My sister dear?

What end do you propose to serve?
    Pray tell me, if you please."
Says TRUTH: " I find I'm here *to freeze;*
For all I meet upon the road,
Deny me shelter or abode.
I'm shunn'd as if in fear or hate;
But that, alas! must be the fate
Of dames, like me, when out of date."
" Not so," says FABLE in reply,
" For you are younger still than I ;
And yet, if I may be believ'd,
I'm ev'rywhere still well receiv'd.
But let me ask, why 'tis that you
Expose your nakedness to view?
That's not discreet.   Now list to me,
Since well our int'rests do agree :
Let my broad mantle drape your form :
'Twill serve to shelter both from harm.
Among the wise, for your sake,
All will my foolish sayings take ;
And with the fools, because of me,
You always well receiv'd will be."
Thus FABLE, side by side with TRUTH,
Like as two sisters, hand in hand,
Will teach and please both age and youth,
And welcom'd be in ev'ry land.

FABLE II.

THE MIRROR OF TRUTH.

In that fam'd time, the age of gold,
When peace prevail'd in every land,
And simple TRUTH herself made bold
To rove at large with glass in hand,
Each in her mirror dar'd to trace,
Without a blush, his own true face.

But crimes and vices stole in fast,
And soon those happy days were past.
Then TRUTH, disgusted, to Heaven flew,
And back to earth her mirror threw.
Alas! 'twas broken in the fall,
And scatter'd wide and lost to all.

Long centuries after it was seen
How very great the loss had been ;
And wise men then began with care
To seek out where the fragments were.
They sometimes find them, here and there,
But very small and very rare :
So that they prove of little worth.
The truest man of all the earth,
With strongest mind and purest heart,
Can see himself therein but part.

FABLE III.

THE THREE RIVALS.

ONCE on a time rose fierce disputes
Between three very gentle brutes—
     The ox, the horse, and ass.
Their overweening pride, alas!
As oft with men of seeming sense,
Led them to strive for precedence.
Perhaps, my friend, you may deride
The thought of asses having pride;
But are not others sometimes vain,
And aim at rank they can't attain?

The patient ox with humble mien,
Describ'd what worker he had been ;
     How great his strength ;
     And then at length
Dwelt on his great docility.
The courser boasted of his worth,
His noble carriage and his birth ;
The ass of his utility.
" Let's leave the question to three men ;
For here they come," exclaimed the horse ;
" If two decide for one, why then
We'll yield the palm to him of course."
The ox, who bore an honest face,
Was charged to plainly state the case,
     And ask for judgment thereupon.
One of the men a jockey was,
And therefore plead the horse's cause,
     Because the horse could run.
" Nay, nay, my friend, it is not so,"
One of the men—a cartman—said,
" The horse is only fit for show :
I put the useful ass ahead."
" Oh, what great folly !" said the third,
" Whoever falser notions heard ?
'Tis plain to farmers of good sense,
The ox should have the preference."
" What !" said the courser in a huff,
" Judgment like this is merest stuff !
'Tis interest that rules with you."
" Pooh !" said the jockey, " that is true ;
But is it something strange or new ?"

FABLE IV.

THE TWO TRAVELERS.

Two friendly comrades, Tom and Bill,
Were on their way to Thionville,
When Thomas found
A purse of gold upon the ground.
"What a wind-fall for us!" said Bill.

" No, not for us," Tom quick replies :
" To me, alone, belongs the prize."
Bill answered not.   But soon their way
Led them where ambush'd robbers lay.
Tom, trembling, would have taken flight.
But rivetted by his affright,
Exclaimed, " Alas ! we are undone !"
" Not we," says Bill, " but you alone."
And saying so he nimbly flies.
And through a hedge securely hies.
But Tom is captur'd, gagg'd, and bound,
And robb'd of all the gold he'd found.

Who, like our hero, is inclined
  To keep good luck for his own ends.
Must soon or late be doom'd to find,
  When ill luck comes he'll have no friends.

FABLE V.

THE INQUISITIVE CAT.

Ye bold philosophers who strain
Th' inexplicable to explain,
Deign but to listen while I tell
What once a curious cat befell.

This tabby one day chanced to pass
Before her master's toilette glass ;
And made an effort to come at

What seemed to her a stranger cat.
Failing in front the cat to find,
She slyly then stole round behind.
Not meeting there the cat she sought,
And almost to her wit's ends brought,
Yet bent the mystery to explore,
  She mounted on the glass astride,
One paw behind and one before
  And in that way to catch it tried.

Now, bending down, an ear she spies,
And then another, which she eyes;
Then with spry movements, quick and deft,
Working her paws from right to left,
She strives to grab the fleeting shade.
The shadows still her grasp evade,
  Till, losing balance, down she went—
Down from the table to the floor—
Resolv'd to hunt for shades no more,
  But with plain sense to be content.

Turning away from things so nice.
She left the glass and went for mice.
"For what," thought she, "can be the use
Pursuing matters so abstruse?"
Involv'd in snares without an end,
Which none can ever comprehend,
Let wise philosophers discuss,
What has no use for them or us.

FABLE VI

THE CARP AND HER YOUNG.

"Take care, my little ones, take care,
Beware the river's bank," she said,
"The treach'rous hook is lurking there;
The hawk is hov'ring in the air;
Keep ever to the river's bed."
Thus 'midst the waters of the Seine,
The carp once plead, yet plead in vain,

With her young fry.
'Twas April; and through all the sky,
The warm and moisty zephyrs flew,
To wake the mountains from their dreams;
And fill again the languid streams,
Which overflow'd the country through.
  Oh then to see
  The revelry
  Of the young fry,
  As brisk and spry,
They darted through the swollen flood!
  " Where's now your fear,
  My mother dear?
 There's nothing here but good.
The flood is to a deluge grown,
The whole world now is overflown,
And its dominion is our own.
What is the need, midst such a sea,
In fear of hooks or hawks to be?"
Thus said the young fry in their glee.
" No, no," the mother straight replies,
" This flood is but a moment's rise;
Your only safety, as I've said,
Is not to leave the river's bed."
  " Oh pish!"
Exclaimed the mad young fish.
  " You weak old carp!
You always on that one string harp!
We are resolv'd to leave the Seine,
And enter on our new domain."

So saying, off the young ones go,
Exulting in the overflow.
We need not on their journey dwell,
For soon the risen waters fell ;
The carplings, caught in shallow pools,
                The fools !
Were hurried to the frying pan.
Now let him tell me, he who can,
Why did these carplings disobey,
And from the river stroll away ?
Was it because they thought they knew
Their mother's counsels were not true ?
Or was't they wanted something new ?
Or did they think that—Ah, my friend !
To such inquiries where's the end ?

FABLE VII.

THE TWO GARDENERS.

Two brother gardeners had the lot
To fall heirs to a garden spot.
They halved in peace the legacy,
Working together day by day,
Living in perfect amity,
Each managing in his own way.
One of the two, whose name was John,

A gift of speech much doted on.
He thought himself a man of wit.
That e'en for LL.D. was fit.

He had the knack
Of conning o'er the almanac.
Of books and charts he kept a stock,
And daily eyed the weather-cock.
Still to his genius giving wing,

He sought to know
How from one single pea could spring
The thousand peas that from it grow ;—
Why from the linden's tiny seed
A tree so lofty should proceed,
While from the bean's far ampler size
A mere shrub comes that shortly dies ;
And, above all, how beans should know
Their branches up from earth to throw,
Yet downwards thrust their roots below.
But while in search of truths like these,
He quite forgets his cabbages.

His wat'ring pot
Is too forgot.
He fails his fig-trees to protect,
Against the cold north winds that freeze,
While wilted drops his lettuces,
And all things suffer from neglect.
He has no fruit ; and, what is worse,
There is no money in his purse ;
So that our learned doctor lacks,
In spite of all his almanacs,

The means wherewith to live,
And fain must take what others give.

His brother, up at break of day,
Went to his work with right good will;
Sung with the birds a cheerful lay,
And never failed his lot to till.
Setting aside the things unknown,
And mindful of his crops alone,
In simple faith he sow'd his field,
And was rewarded by the yield.
He dug and water'd ev'rything,
From gooseberry to apricot:
And none to market e'er could bring
Of fruits and plants a finer lot.
Hence he had money and to spare,
And with his brother well could share.
"How is't," said John, "my brother dear,
That you know how to thrive so well?"
His brother answered: "'Tis quite clear;
We need not on the myst'ry dwell.
I go to work and till the ground,
While *you* do naught but rack your brains;
And while with *me* all things abound,
You get but labor for your pains.
The question, then, I leave to you,
Which is the wiser of the two?"

FABLE VIII.

THE GARDENER AND THE AGED TREE.

A tree that in a garden stood,
 Had grown too old for doing good :
  Such is the fate of all.
It was a pear-tree that no more

Its former luscious fruitage bore :
 And hence was doom'd to fall.
Scarce had th' ungrateful gardener sunk
His sharp-edged axe into its trunk,
 When thus the old tree spoke:—
" Oh think of all the good I've done ;
The fruit I've borne ; the praise I've won,
 And spare the murd'rous stroke !
Oh do not hasten to their end
The few last days of your old friend ! "
The ingrate answer'd :—" Yea, indeed,
I'm truly loath to lay you low ;
But still of wood I stand in need,
And cannot to the forest go."
The nightingales then intercede ;
Gush out a long and loud refrain,
And of th' intended wrong complain.
They wake the gardener's memory—
His wife oft sitting 'neath that tree,
And list'ning to their song the while
Their dulcet notes her cares beguile.
But he, unheeding their appeal,
Resolv'd another blow to deal.
The aged trunk the stroke broke in,
Which rais'd around his ears a din.
For out there came a swarm of bees,
And gave th' intruder words like these :—
" What are you doing, wretched man ?
Your int'rests inj'ring all you can !
Are you not able to perceive

That if this home to us you'd leave,
Our honey of more worth would be
Than all the wood of this old tree?
All tender memories apart,
Does not this reason reach your heart?"
"Ah, yes!" the gardener said at last.
"What happy days have here been past!
Much do I owe this good old tree
For all the fruit 't has given me.
How oft my wife has hither stray'd,
To sit beneath its soothing shade,
While 'midst its whisp'ring leaves above,
The nightingales recall'd our love!

Yes, let the old tree stand!
And for these bees whose honied store
Will make me richer than before,
With flowers I'll plant the land."

So thus it is, we may rely,
That mankind grateful will be found,
When only ev'ry means we try,
To have them by their int'rests bound.

FABLE IX.

THE IVY AND THE THYME.

" How I do pity you, indeed,
My sorry, little trembling weed ! "
Once said the ivy to the thyme.
" You always creep and never climb,
Whilst scarce above the ground you rise,
I mount this oak and seek the skies :—
The old oak which Jove cherishes,
    My comrade is."

" I know," the thyme replied, " 'tis true,
In height I can't dispute with you,
But my support is all my own,
While you could never stand alone.
'Tis by that tree you mount so high ;
Alone you could not climb at all ;
But in your feebleness would fall,
    And creep e'en lower than I."

Attend ye authors who would seek
By learned Latin, or by Greek,
To climb aloft in prose or rhyme :—
    Whate'er you do,
    Keep well in view,
These words of wisdom of the thyme.

FABLE X.

THE CHILD AND THE LOOKING-GLASS.

Once on a time it came to pass,
    A child by a poor woman rais'd,
First saw at home a looking-glass,
    In which it often fondly gazed.

At length, by a mere child's caprice,
    But which the grown man often shows,
Its raptures for the mirror cease,
    At which it ugly glances throws.

These glances now his rage inflame,
  At what he loved before:
And as the image makes the same,
  He's angered more and more.

Whene'er his angry fist he shakes,
Or wry and hateful faces makes,
The image, aping ev'ry whim,
Repeats the same bad thoughts to him.

Enraged at insults so extreme,
At last he bursts out in a scream.

His mother coming wiped his face.
And gave her child a kind embrace;
Consol'd his wrath and gently show'd
How 'twas those insults were bestowed.

" For, if you smile," she said, " 'tis plain,
The image will smile back again.
Extend your arms for an embrace,
And 'twill not make an angry face.
You see, whatever you may do,
The image does the same to you."

So in the world at large 'twill be;
'Tis your own image there you'll see.

FABLE XI.

THE TWO CATS.

Two cats of ancient pedigree,
The finest of their race e'er seen,
Were diff'rent in a great degree,
For one was fat and 'tother lean.
The elder daily had a feast,
Like senator, or judge, or priest;
Was round and portly, fresh, and sleek,

Serene of brow, and plump of cheek,
While 'tother, eating mice alone,
Was little else than skin and bone;
Though ever busy on the watch,
As cats should be, his prey to catch,
Peering around with famish'd look,
In ev'ry cranny, hole, and nook,
He toil'd from morn till eve, and yet
Could scarce a full meal ever get.
At length, by hunger sore distress'd,
His elder brother he address'd :—
" How is't that *you* can have good cheer,
While *I* at death's door am so near?
Though you are idle all the day,
And I'm at work, and never play,
How is it, brother, please explain,
Why you are fat and I am lean?"
" The reason, brother, 's very plain,"
Said fatty in complacent strain,
You've quite too conscientious been.
You hunt for mice."   " Is that not right?"
The younger answered with some spite.
" Ah, yes," the elder makes reply.
" 'Tis right enough, perhaps, but I
Can always near my master sit,
And seek to please him by my wit.
I share his favors, his repast :
Ask little first, take much at last :
Strive to amuse him with my tricks,
Learn'd in the school of politics,

While you, my brother, are a flat,
And serve him merely as a cat.
The real secret of success,
In cunning lies, not usefulness.
If you would prosper here below,
Play tricks and let your duties go!"

FABLE XII.

THE PRINCE AND THE NIGHTINGALE.

A young prince and his tutor stray'd
Through a grove for a promenade.
There, as the time upon him hung
    With heavy weight—
(Such is the usage of the great),
A bird beneath the foliage sung:
It was the charming nightingale.
Should not the princely rank avail
To cage the bird without delay?
But hunting through the leafy shade,
So great the fracas that he made,
The bird took fright and flew away.

"Why," said His Highness, in great wrath—
"Why does this bird thus shun my path?
Why does he choose this desert waste,
While sparrows round my palace feast?"

His tutor answer'd:—"This will show
What some day you will come to know;
Fools crowd in plenty to be bought,
While merit hides, and must be sought."

FABLE XIII.

TRUE HAPPINESS.

A poor young cricket, small and shy,
Passing retir'd his summer hours,
Beheld one day a butterfly,
      Flitting among the flowers.
Of ev'ry color, ev'ry hue,

The gaudy insect well might boast.
From flower to flower it gaily flew,
Alighting where it pleas'd him most.
"Alas!" the pining cricket sigh'd,
"What diff'rences us two divide!
While Nature does so much for him,
For me she nothing does at all.
I'm void of sense and coarse of limb,
With figure despicably small;
I'm heeded not, am lone and lorn,
And might as well have not been born."
But while the cricket thus complain'd,
A sudden uproar round him reign'd;
A troop of children rushing by,
Came hunting for the butterfly.
With nets, and hats, and kerchiefs too,
The gaudy insect they pursue.
He struggles hard to get away,
But falls at last a helpless prey.
One seizes on his wings of gold;
Another at his body aims;
A third upon his head lays hold;
In short, each one the insect claims,
But leaves him mangled, dead, and cold.
"Ah, ha!" the cricket said, "I see
What 'tis a brilliant thing to be.
If such the cost to those who shine,
I ought no longer to repine;
But to live happy I must be
Contented with obscurity."

FABLE XIV.

THE SHEPHERD AND THE NIGHTINGALE.

One balmy night in charming May,
As on a hill a shepherd lay,
And from the sky with stars o'erspread,
The moon her silv'ry radiance shed ;
While from the rose and lilacs there,
Perfumes were filling all the air;
While meadows all asleep and still,
Were lull'd by murmurs of the rill,
A nightingale with tender strain,
Voic'd forth the peace of hill and plain,
Which seem'd uprising to the skies,
From Nature's sweetest harmonies.
But in the fullness of that peace,
Then all at once the warblings cease.
The bird had ended her wild song,
And would no more its strains prolong.
The shepherd urged her, but in vain,
To sing that witching song again.
" No," said the bird, " my days are o'er ;
These scenes shall hear my voice no more.

For do you not, from yonder bogs,
Hear the loud discord of those frogs,
Who drown my music by their din,
With which mine own cannot begin ?
Before their mastery I yield,
And must forever quit the field."
" Nay," said the shepherd, " that's the way
To give those croakers their full sway.
To silence you is what they want,
And strive to do it by that rant.
When I am hearing *your* sweet airs,
I'm not e'en conscious then of theirs."

FABLE XV

THE LAUGHING SOLITAIRE.

Throughout all Greece 'twas known
That Mysone lived alone—
That he lov'd wisdom for herself ;
Was free from trouble as from pelf ;
Content and easy, without strife,
Reflecting on the things of life.

In woods retir'd he pass'd his days,
Far from the crowd's accustom'd ways.
    But in this solitude,
Where nothing trivial might intrude,
He would at times quite jovial be,
And laugh out loud and merrily.
At length one day two Grecians came,
Attracted by his laughing fame,
And in amazement wish'd to know
How any mortal living so,
Could laugh. " How can you laugh, Mysone,"
They ask'd, " since you live all alone ? "
" That is the very reason why
I laugh," was his reply.

FABLE XVI.

THE TWO YOUNG WARRIORS.

Two farmer-boys, genteel and bright,
Who in ill-doing took delight
(For they were by their father spoil'd),
Were seeking nests the garden round.
A brood of partridges they found,
And in their joy went nearly wild.
The fledgelings scatter far and near
Under the impulse of their fear,

FLORIAN'S FABLES.

And to go free great efforts make ;
But the two urchins here and there,
Meet and head them everywhere,
Till every single one they take.
The mother trails her wings in vain ;
Now timid flies, and now makes bold ;
But uselessly she'd longer feign :
The boys get all their pockets hold.
Each boy has six ; one yet remains ;
And for this odd one both contend :
Each of his rights and wrongs complains,
Till of dispute there seems no end.
"Let us draw lots!" "No!" "Yes!" "Yes!" "No!"
    So to and fro,
The bandied words between them go.
    " I'll knock you down !"
    " I'll break your crown !"
Hot and hotter the contest grew,
When th' older one the odd bird threw
    At his brother's head.
The younger brother in reply,
Then let another birdling fly.
The elder back another sped.
    Neither will yield,
Until the ground is strewn around
    Like any battle field,
With quiv'ring, gasping, dying birds.
The father, hap'ning round that way,
Stopp'd to observe the cruel play,
And to his boys address'd these words :—

" What! are you *kings*, that you should be
With lives of innocents so free ?
What right have you, I'd like to know,
To deal around you death and woe,
Like emperors, whose sport it is,
To slay mankind like partridges ? "

FABLE XVII.

THE FOX AS A PREACHER.

An old fox, gouty, apoplectic,
All broken down, but learn'd and wise,
Eloquent and skill'd in logic,
His art at moral teaching tries,
And to the desert rais'd his cries.
His style was fine, his moral good :
Under three heads his sermons stood ;
He plainly prov'd simplicity,
Good manners and integrity,
Must end in that felicity
To which a lying world allures,
But never to our hopes secures,
Although we pay for't a large fee.
At first he met with no success :
None ever came to hear him preach,
Save a few squirrels, more or less,
Who chanc'd to fall within his reach ;
Or timid does, of little name,
Who could not spread the preacher's fame.
At length he wholly chang'd his course,
And aim'd at tyrants his discourse.

THE FOX AS A PREACHER.

With lofty strokes he boldly dares
To hit at lions, tigers, bears,
And all the monsters of the wood :
Condemns their ravenous thirst for blood,
Their gluttony, their rage, their spite.

Their love of wrong, contempt of right,
The selfish use they make of war,
    Et cetera, et cetera.
And now the world crowd up to hear
A preacher of so little fear.
Deer, gazelles, kids, show their deep sense
Of his all-powerful eloquence.
His gen'rous truths they recognize:
He's listened to with weeping eyes;
His fame is spread the country round;
The tidings far and near resound—
Are borne upon the pop'lar voice,
Until at court they make a noise.
The lion who at that time reign'd
(Good and pious as things then went),
To hear the famous preacher deign'd,
And to invite his presence sent.
Charm'd with the royal courtesy,
The preacher went without delay.
His sermon now himself surpass'd.
It was a perfect thunder-blast
Against th' infernal thirst for blood
Indulged by tyrants of the wood.
He spoke of helpless innocence,
Oppress'd by lawless insolence:
Dwelt on the vices of the great:
Their love of power insatiate:
He call'd for justice long delay'd,
'Gainst those who on the feeble prey'd,
Till beasts of prey all quak'd with fear

Such awful sentences to hear.
The courtier's at each other gaz'd,
And at such rudeness sat amaz'd ;
But prudently remarks forbore.
Because the king was pleas'd to be,
Complacent towards this liberty,
Accustom'd to such things before.
The sermon ended, the king sent
To manifest his great content.
Had the bold preacher to him brought,
And thank'd him for the truths he'd taught.
" What must I give you in reward,"
He ask'd, " for fearless words like these ? "
Old Reynard, taken off his guard,
Replied :—" Some turkeys if you please ! "

FABLE XVIII.

THE KING OF PERSIA.

Once on a time a Persian king
With all his court was at the chase.
Becoming dry, he found no spring,
Nor any water in the place.
But near at hand a garden lay,
With citrons, grapes and oranges,
Whose juices might his thirst allay.
" But God save me from eating these ! "
The king exclaim'd ; " for if one fruit
I take from out that garden wall,
These viziers mine would follow suit,
And take fruit, trees, and garden all."

FABLE XIX.

THE RHINOCEROS AND DROMEDARY.

One day a young rhinoceros
    Thus address'd the dromedary :—
"Can you, my friend, explain to us
    Why our fortunes so much vary—

Why man the lord of all our race
Always provides for you a place?
He gives you shelter, food, and care;
And e'en his bread with you will share.
By him you are esteem'd so high,
He seeks your race to multiply.
You have good qualities, 'tis true;
Are gentle, sober, never slack:
You bear his burdens on your back,
     His wife and children too:
       All this I own:
But are these merits yours alone?
To *us* then, is there nothing due?
In fact, I think, with due respect,
We well might man's regards expect
       As well as you.
We furnish him with horn and shield
To aid him on the battle-field.
Yet he pursues us with his hate;
Hunts us with rage insatiate;
Despises us, or in his wrath,
Impels us to avoid his path."

The dromedary made reply:—
" Why envy us our lot, my friend?
To serve is nothing: you must try
To make man's pleasure your sole end.
Be not surpris'd that he should show
     Such favor to our progeny:
The secret of it, you must know,
     Is this:—we've learn'd to bend the knee."

FABLE XX.

THE PEACOCK, TWO GOSLINGS, AND THE DIVER.

His wondrous plumes the peacock spread,
And was admir'd by other birds;

But two young geese in mud-holes bred,
Quawk'd out their comments in these words:—
" Do see," said one, " that leg of his !
And what an ugly foot that is ! "
" And what a voice ! " the other cried,
" Enough to make the scritch-owl hide."
So pleas'd were they with their own wit,
They went into a laughing fit.
When of a sudden up there came
A diver from the depths below.
" Messieurs ! " said he, " though you may blame
The bird for faults that we all know,
Yet is your voice than his more sweet,
Or have you any better feet,
That you should venture thus to quiz ?
And as for plumage, let me say,
You never yet will see the day,
When yours will equal his."

FABLE XXI

THE MISER AND HIS SON.

By what strange chance I do not know,
But on a time it happened so—
A miser to the market went,
And a small sum for apples spent.

Plac'd in a closet in a row,
They make a most delightful show,
He counts and counts them o'er and o'er,
Then double-locks and bolts the door,
Yet oft returns to view his store.

But sad indeed this miser's lot,
For even miser's apples rot:
He sighing eats the ones that perish,
But still persists the sound to cherish.

His son, a school-boy, on half fare,
Discover'd where the apples were:
He got the keys, and with two friends,
For his short fare soon made amends.

The miser came and stood dismayed
To see the havoc they had made,
He loud exclaim'd as if undone,
"Give back my apples every one,
Or I'll hang ev'ry mother's son!"

"Be quiet, father," said the boy,
"We are all decent fellows here;
So be appeas'd and do not fear;
We would not in the least annoy:
We leave the bad ones for your sake,
'Tis only sound ones that we take."

FABLE XXII.

THE OLD MAN'S ADVICE.

"Please teach me how a fortune's made,"
A young man to his father said.
The old man answer'd:—"There's a way
Which is glorious, I may say:
Though 'tis the way least understood;—
It is to serve the common good;
To give one's life, one's toil, one's care
In useful service of the state."
"Oh that's a labor far too great:
I want some way less hard by far."
"Well then, there's intrigue, which is sure."
"But that vile way I can't endure.
From both hard labor and from vice
     I would be freed'd."
"Then be a fool! Take my advice;—
For many such I've seen succeed."

FABLE XXIII.

THE ROPE-DANCER.

A young man on the tight-rope danc'd
     With balance-pole in hand;
Sway'd to and fro, fell back, advanc'd,
     Or bolt up straight would stand.
A crowd of persons came to see,
His feats of bold agility.
Now up he goes, then down again,
All free and easy, light and spry;
Rebounding from the tight rope's strain,
In cadence with it springing high.

THE ROPE-DANCER.

As birds that o'er the water go,
But barely touch it with the wing,
So he but seem'd to press the toe
Upon the quick-responding string.

Of these exploits grown proud at length,
He said one day :—" Why use this pole ?
It weighs me down, impairs my strength,
Embarrasses my free control—
More grace I'd have and freer play
If I should throw the thing away."
    No sooner said than done.
But once his pole was thrown aside,
And his new dancing had begun,
With arms outstretch'd and awkward stride,
He waver'd, lost his balance, fell,
Broke his nose, and all the crowd
At his tumble laughed aloud.

My dear young friends ! you know full well
That he who has no check at all,
Must soon or later have a fall.
Though reason, virtue, rule, and law
Against young inclinations draw
    Like a check-rein,
Your fiery passions to restrain ;
They are the needed balance-pole,
To keep your fame and fortune whole.

FABLE XXIV.

THE MONKEY AND THE APE.

A young ape one day found a nut,
Which straight into his mouth he put,
And set his teeth on't for a bite.
He tried it o'er and o'er again,

But finding all his efforts vain,
Threw it away with spite.
"My mother must have lied," he said,
"To say she had on such things fed—
    That they were good and sweet,
      And fit to eat.
What fools are young folks to believe
Old women's tales—they but deceive!
    The devil take such fruit,
      And granny too, to boot!"
A monkey seizing on the prize,
Thus to the foolish ape replies:—
"See here! my friend, I'll show to you,
That your good mother told you true."
Then with a stone the nut he breaks,
And therefrom all the kernel takes.
      And as he eats
      Its luscious sweets—
"You see," says he, "for food 'tis fit,
If you'll take pains to open it.
No good in this life one e'er gains,
Without some labor, care, and pains."

FABLE XXV.

THE LINNET AND THE TURTLE DOVE.

A little linnet all day long
Found constant happiness in song,
The while her friend, a turtle dove,
Nor thought nor car'd for aught but love.
"You're very wrong," the turtle said,

" To waste your time in such a way ;
The greatest pleasure for a maid
Is to have lovers ev'ry day :
What song can e'er impart the bliss
The lover feels from one sweet kiss?"
To this the linnet warbl'd low :—
" I could not venture to compare
One with the other ; but I know
How great the charms of music are :
        If these I have,
No other pleasure do I crave."
At this discourse, the dove in spite
Bade her adieu, and took to flight.

Years pass'd, ten long and weary years,
With all their checker'd hopes and fears,
When one fine day in spring the twain
Met in the same old grove again.
Great was the change they'd undergone,
        And long they stood and gaz'd,
            As if amaz'd
At looks so alter'd and forlorn.

At length the linnet silence broke,
        And thus politely spoke :—
" Good morning, friend ! How do you do ?
And how are all those lovers too ?"
" Ah ! never mention them, my dear :
For I have lost them all, I fear :
Friends, lovers, youth, and pleasures—yea,
Everything has pass'd away.

To love and please was all my thought;
But what delusion it has brought!
I still love on, just as before,
But then I'm lov'd in turn no more."

" I'm not so badly off as you,"
The linnet said ; " for though 'tis true
I'm growing old, with loss of voice,
Yet still in music I rejoice,
And when with her wild magic trills
The nightingale the forest fills,
Beguiling all the weary night,
Her sweet song fills me with delight."

Though beauty is a gift divine,
Yet its possession may not bless;
Its charms with merit must combine
To prove a source of happiness :
   It fades away,
   While talents stay
And please e'en when our own decay.

HERCULES IN HEAVEN.

When Hercules, his labors done,
For his reward had Heaven won,
The gods pressed forward to salute
A hero of such wide repute.
Minerva, Mars, and Venus came
To show their rev'rence for his name;
E'en Juno's self was quite polite
Which fill'd the hero with delight.
But when with those assembled there
God Plutus came with lofty air,
And gave his hand with haughty pride,
Our hero turn'd his head aside.

"My son!" said Jupiter, "say why
Such anger flashes from thine eye.
What has this god e'er done to thee
That thou with him so wroth shouldst be?"

"It is because I know him well:
When I upon the earth did dwell,
I saw him going hand in hand,
With the worst knaves of all the land."

FABLE XXVII.

THE PHILOSOPHER AND THE OWL.

Wroug'd, persecuted, and proscrib'd,
In foreign lands compell'd to hide,
For calling things by their right name,
A sage took with him all his wealth—
(His wisdom)—which he kept by stealth,
    And to a friendly forest came.

There, while pond'ring o'er his woes,
He saw an owl beset by foes—
An angry crowd of jays and crows.
They peck'd him, curs'd him, call'd him sot,
And said he was no patriot.
" Let's pluck him," said they, " of his plumes—
This rascal who such wit assumes ! "
" Let's hang him," said the wrathful birds,
" And judge the villain afterwards ! "

In vain the owl implor'd for peace,
And call'd on them their rage to cease.
The sage was touch'd to see the owl
Assail'd by words and deeds so foul
(For wisdom always makes the mind
To peace and gentleness inclin'd).
He quell'd the rage, and ask'd the bird
Why such a mob was 'gainst him stirr'd.
" Wherefore," said he, " is all this strife ?
Why do these foes thus seek your life ? "
" My only crime," the owl replied,
" Is one which they cannot abide :
The reason why I've rous'd their spite,
Is simply this—I see by night."

FABLE XXVIII.

THE LEOPARD AND THE MONKEYS.

Once on a time some monkey folk
    Hot-cockles play'd.
The game was but a simple joke:
A fair one sits, her lap array'd
So as to hide a monkey's eyes:

He holds his paw to catch a blow;
Who gives the blow he does not know,
But all his wit at guessing tries.
Does he guess wrong? Oh, then how great
The laughter, frolic, and the fun,
    The cry, the frisk, the escapade,
    The hop, the skip, the gambolade
That through the crowd of players run!

Drawn by the noise a leopard came
And enter'd on the sportive scene.
They trembled at his very name,
Though of a gentle air and mien.
"Be not disturb'd," his lordship said:
"I would in no wise incommode;
With no ill aim do I invade
The premises of your abode:
Let me with you enjoy your fun:
    Please let the sport go on."
"Ah, sir, how good it is of you,
To honor poor folks as you do!
What! you a man of high degree,
Thus set aside your dignity,
And join with folks so plain as we!"
    "Yes, such is my philosophy.
It is my fancy to declare,
That animals all equal are;
So let the play go on, I say;
    Yes, let us have the play."

Delighted by his words so fair,

As by fair words folks always are,
The crowd believes as others do,
And once again their sports renew.
One hides his eyes, his hand extends,
As formerly among his friends,
And straight the leopard deals a blow
That makes the crimson blood to flow.

This time the monkey well could guess
Whose blow had given him such distress;
But waiting not the name to say,
He in great silence stole away.
His comrades vainly strove to smile;
The leopard howe'er laugh'd outright;
They all excus'd themselves the while,
        As best they might.
And leaving, thus growl'd out their spite:—
" The people of such lofty tone
'Twere well for us to let alone ;
For hid beneath the softest paws,
The gentlest of them have sharp claws."

FABLE XXIX.

THE TWO BALD-HEADS.

By chance two bald-head beggars found
A something shining in the ground :
 Each strove to have the prize.
They fought, and fought, with kicks and blows :

Pull'd hair and tore their ragged clothes,
  And black'd each other's eyes.

He who at last the object gain'd,
Lost his few locks that still remain'd;
And when his prize he look'd upon,
Lo! 'twas a broken comb he'd won!

THE TWO PEASANTS.

" Bill!" said Luke one cloudy day,
  In a sad foreboding tone,
" Just look at yonder cloud, I pray!
  How very black 'tis grown!
Such threat'ning clouds as that portend
  Some awful end."
" Why?" answer'd Bill, " why think you so?
'Twill only be a common blow."
" Why!" replied Luke in a great pet;
" It is a hail storm, and I'll bet
'Twill ruin vineyards, barley, wheat,
And ev'ry thing we raise to eat.
Nothing to live on will remain:
Famine will follow, and in train
The pest will come, and we shall fall,
Village, people, crops and all!"
  " The pest seize on your storm!"
Said Bill, getting rather warm;
  " Don't take alarm!
For rest assur'd, the world, my friend,

THE TWO PEASANTS.

Is not yet coming to an end;
But contrary to what *you* say,
'Twill still move on from day to day.
'Tis not a hail-cloud that you see:
   A simple rain-storm it will be.

'Twill water ev'ry field
That's suff'ring now for rain;
And great will be the yield
Of ev'ry kind of grain.
A double crop of hay
Our labor will repay:
Wheat, half as much again;
And grapes will load the plain:
We shall lack nothing, I opine,
But casks enough to hold the wine.
        And hence,
We all shall live in opulence."
        "That's very bright!"
        Said Luke with spite.
"Well! my ideas, say what you will,
Are good as yours," responded Bill.
"Oh then," said Luke, "if that's the case,
Let's wait and see what will take place.
You'd better be not quite so fast:
'Tis he laughs best who laughs the last."
"Then God be prais'd!" was Bill's reply,
"*I* shall not be the one to *cry!*"
The two thus heated, and in rage,
A battle were about to wage,
When suddenly a puff of wind,
Bore the portentous cloud away,
Which neither hail'd nor rain'd that day,
        Nor left a trace behind.

FABLE XXXI.

THE LAW-SUIT BETWEEN TWO FOXES.

Oh how I hate that pedant art,
So captious and so very smart,
Which of a thing as clear as light,
Makes all obscure and dark as night;
Makes error right, and proves to you
That truth itself must be untrue!

Th' invention of this art belongs
To folks once skill'd in all such wrongs,
The subtle Greeks, who—may they get
All the reward for't due them yet !

This art an old fox once profess'd ;—
Its perfect master stood confess'd.
He kept a school to teach the way,
And took fat pullets for his pay.
One of his pupils aim'd to be
A lawyer of the first degree,
And for tuition did agree
Of case first gain'd to give the fee.
In legal form the two compact ;
Sign'd, seal'd, deliver'd is the act.
But when the course of study's done,
The pupil for injunction sues ;
Declares he owes his master none
Of all the pullets claim'd for dues.
The leopard, learned in the laws,
Presides as judge to hear the cause.
" May't please the court," the pupil cried,
" If my case's gain'd, I need not pay ;
For so your honor will decide ;
And we the sentence must obey.
And if I lose, why, nothing's due,
For the conditions plainly say,
'Tis only if I win I pay.
Such is the law I apprehend ;
I would not, truly, wrong my friend."

" Nay, nay, not so," the master said,
" The law is clear upon that head ;
For should the case against you go,
Then you should pay the debt you owe.
And if you win, why, then indeed
You must pay up, as you agreed."

Here rested counsel its defense.
The leopard sat in mute suspense ;
And by the workings of his face
He seem'd confounded with the case.
But finally he silence broke,
And thus his sentence briefly spoke :—
" In this sharp case the court must rule
The master no more keeps his school ;
And to the pupil—this award,—
From future practice he's debar'd."

FABLE XXXII.

THE VIPER AND THE BLOOD-SUCKER.

Once to the leech the viper said—
    " How different is our lot !
They who love you would wish *me* dead;
    Men like me not.
They seem to bear for me some spite,

While on their blood they let you feed.
Like you, I only give a bite;
I do, like you, but make them bleed."

" But my dear friend," the leech replied,
" *I* bite to heal, but *you* to kill;
How many patients would have died
But for the virtue of my skill !
While well men are destroy'd by you,
The health of sick men I renew.
The difference 'tween us is, in chief,
Your bite is poison, *mine*, relief."

My tale would thus hold up to view,
What few have fail'd to see, I wist—
The leech presents the Critic true;
The viper is the Satirist.

FABLE XXXIII

THE LEARNED COLLEGIANS.

An owl drawn from his hiding-place
By students in pursuit of knowledge,
Was made to show his sapient face
Within the precincts of a college.
There quarter'd with a cat and goose,
He of the privilege made use
To go with them the whole course through.

Herodotus by heart they knew,
Denis of Halicarnassus too ;
And all that Titus Livy wrote
Like learned doctors they could quote.
Discussing once as doctors do,
They pass'd the ancients in review.

" Upon my faith," the cat exclaim'd,
" The Egyptians were of all most fam'd.
No people ever were more wise,
More law-abiding or discreet—
None more religious 'neath the skies :
For that alone I think it meet
That Egypt should bear off the prize."

The owl responded : " In my view,
To Athens the first prize is due.
Whoever knew such wit, such grace,
Such bravery in any race ?
No state more noble men e'er bore,
Or with less means accomplish'd more.
Of all the nations Greece rank'd first."

" Hold there ! " the goose in wrath outspoke,
" You reckon Rome, then, last and worst !
Perhaps, my friends, you are in joke.
What nation ever equall'd Rome ?
In grandeur, glory, arts, and war,
Egypt and Greece can't near it come.
All nations it excell'd by far :
The men of Rome *my* fav'rites are.
They conquer'd on both land and sea :

To this, at least, you must agree."

But while the pedants thus debate,
They each become more obstinate,
Until a rat who had much wit
From eating learned manuscript,
 Cried to the crew :—
" I see why each should hold his view :
In Egypt men ador'd the cat ;
The Athenians worship'd owls ;
The Romans petted and made fat
 The goose as first of fowls.
As your self-int'rest points the way,
So your opinions turn and sway."

FABLE XXXIV.

THE CROCODILE AND STURGEON.

Upon the banks of ancient Nile,
Two urchins stopp'd to play awhile :
Over the waters smooth, profound,
They made flat pebbles skip and bound.
But soon an end's put to their play—
A crocodile disturbs their fun :
He seizes, crushes, swallows one,

While 'tother runs away.
A sturgeon saw the murd'rous deed,
And hasten'd off with all his speed—
From horror at the act he fled,
To hide deep in the river's bed.
But there, amidst distressing fears,
Strange, unexpected news he hears—
The crocodile was shedding tears!
Could murd'rers then, with blood still wet,
For their foul deeds feel such regret?
Was he then suff'ring from the stings,
Which true contrition always brings?
And can the gods have the intent
T' avenge, not save, the innocent?
This villain surely now relents,
And of his wickedness repents.
" I'll go to him and tell him true,
What it imports his soul to do."
The honest sturgeon then proceeds
To seek the monster 'midst the reeds.
" Yes, weep," said he, " as well you may,
For this foul deed you've done to-day.
Remorse a balm is, and it heals
The pains a wounded spirit feels.
Then use this balm with thanks and joy,
You monster! thus to eat a boy!
Now that repentance you have felt ;—
Now that in tears your heart does melt,
There's yet relief from all your fears."
" Pooh !" said the knave, " that I've shed tears

Perhaps is true ;
But not for what I've done to-day,
In that I did but *one* boy slay ;
'Twas that another got away,
Which I had hop'd to swallow too ! "

Such tears as these we may believe
Are often shed when sinners grieve.

FABLE XXXV.

THE CATERPILLAR.

One day the animals began
The silk-worm's wond'rous works to scan.
" What talent," they exclaimed, " she shows !
How glossily her spinning glows !
    How rich, and smooth, and bright ! "
All present her nice thread extoll'd ;
'Twas fine, and soft, and shone like gold,
And well the proudest might delight.

Did we say all ?—No, one there was,
Who in the thread could find some flaws.
It was the caterpillar, who
Was pleas'd to take another view.
With buts, and ifs she seems to doubt,
And hesitates at speaking out.

THE CATERPILLAR.

But why should she thus disagree?
"Oh," cried the fox, "I plainly see;
My lady takes a contr'y view,
Because she is a spinner too."

FABLE XXXVI.

THE JUGGLER.

A mountebank amidst a crowd
    Thus cried aloud—
"Walk up, Messieurs and try the cure
For every evil men endure!
It is a powder which will give
All things for which you strive and live.

To fools it gives intelligence;
And to the guilty innocence.
Honors on rascals it bestows,
And to old women brings young beaux;
Secures old men young, pretty wives;
Makes madmen lead well-temper'd lives—
In short, whatever you would gain,
It will assist you to attain.
  It is a perfect panacea."

The juggler's table I drew near,
This wond'rous powder to behold
Of which such miracles were told.
It was a little powder'd gold !

FABLE XXXVII.

THE GRASSHOPPER.

"'Tis over now, and I must fly!
This odius sight I cannot bear—
The crime, the rage, the misery,
That meet my vision ev'rywhere!
To some obscure retreat I'll go,
Far from abuses, vice, and woe.
The wicked knaves who've cross'd my path,
I'll visit with my studied wrath.

Only because I'd upright be,
I've got the whole world's enmity!
Every man, and child, and beast—
   Yes ev'ry little bird,
   By hate and envy stirr'd,
Do make of me their scand'lous feast.
   Oh base ingratitude!
To treat one thus who is so good.
How little I am understood!
They'll yet regret what they have done;
But only when I'm dead and gone."
Thus in hypochondriac strain,
A grasshopper did once complain.
O'er the world's wrongs he seem'd to groan,
While thinking of himself alone.
A comrade said,—" Holla, my dear!
How did you come by that idea?
Why not enjoy these fields in peace?
They yield for you their rich increase.
   Let the world go,
   And all its woe.
What is't to you, I'd like to know?
'Tis bad and always will be so.
You cannot shape it to your view
By all that you may say or do.
Besides, my friend, where can you find
A world more suited to your mind?
And as to having this world's spite,
I think you are mistaken quite.
It is a fancy, or perchance

Even a touch of arrogance,
That springs from your o'erweening pride,
Rather than any thing beside."
The grasshopper not even deign'd
To make reply when thus arraign'd,
But forthwith from his old home flew,
 To seek a new.
When finally two days were o'er,
He'd made two hundred steps or more,
And fancied that at last he'd found
The end of this world's farthest bound.
The land seem'd new, the people strange,
The wheat-fields offer'd a fine range,
 And fill'd him with delight.
Their long stalks waving in the wind,
Gave welcome to his troubl'd mind;
 It was a glorious sight!
"Here then," he cried, "all trouble past,
I've found security at last.
No more shall enemies invade
My peace within this friendly shade."
  But lo!
When o'er the east spread morning's glow,
A band of reapers came along,
With laugh, and jest, and merry song,
And 'neath their sickles fell the grain
All level with the naked plain;
And to the view the spot disclos'd,
Where our unfortunate repos'd.
"There 'tis again!" the insect cried,

" When *will* my foes be satisfied ?
Turn where I will, I'm still pursu'd,
For having done the world some good !
Scarce have I reach'd this distant land,
When I'm assail'd on ev'ry hand.
These foes come here to seek me out,
And in their mad, infernal rout,
Would almost any means employ,
So that they might my life annoy,
Yes, even their own crops destroy.
I really think to glut their ire,
They'd set their very fields on fire."
Then to the reapers thus he said,—
" Come ! let your wrath fall on my head ;
You've hunted me like thing accurs'd,
And now, Messieurs, just do your worst!"
A busy worker at the sheaf,
By chance observ'd his mighty grief :
He seized him, held him up to view,
Then flung him where bright flowers grew :
" Go !" he exclaim'd, " where posies are ;
Go, little friend, get supper there !"

FABLE XXXVIII.

THE HEDGEHOG AND THE RABBITS.

Some characters are ne'er at ease,
And always must be making war:
They like to sting, and to displease,
And highly gifted at it are.
To *me* they are a perfect pest.
Though they be wise as Solomon,
And have e'en royal garments on,

Yet their rude manners I detest.
The robes of virtue's self should be
          Politeness and civility.
A hedgehog once of evil fame,
Forc'd from his home by some disgrace,
Unto a rabbit-warren came,
Burning with hate against his race.
He told the gentle inmates there,
All that he'd suffer'd everywhere;
Against his foes exhal'd his bile,
And ask'd asylum for a while.
" With pleasure, sir," the leader said,
" You'll here find shelter, board, and bed.
Be one of us ; make free and bold ;
We all things here in common hold.
We simple, frugal people are,
And have no great affairs on hand ;
To crop the clover our chief care,
Or nibble o'er the dewy land.
At the first streak of early dawn,
We're out betimes upon the lawn.
The dangers from our homes to ward,
Each takes his turn in standing guard.
And when the sentry gives alarm,
We're off at once to hide from harm.
Thus with our little ones and wives,
We pass our happy, cheerful lives.
These lives, 'tis true, are oft cut short,
And made of dogs and boys the sport.
But this good reason serves to give

Why we make merry while we live.
We study friendship, love, and peace,
And our enjoyments thus increase.
Life we embellish all we may,
By kind attentions all the day.
If you're content with us to be,
Then come and join our colony.
If not, why then at least you'll stay,
And take your dinner here to-day.
You'd please us with your company."
The hedgehog to these words replied—
" It would, indeed, give me great pride,
With such good people to reside."
Then every rabbit forward press'd,
And civilly their joy express'd,
With offer'd welcome to their guest.
All things went well till night had come,
When discord rent the happy home.
For when at supper they began
For morrow's work to fix the plan,
The hedgehog, bent to have his will,
At a young rabbit shot a quill.
" Excuse me, friend," the father says ;
" I'm not accustom'd to such ways."
This rais'd the bristling hedgehog's ire,
And caus'd him right and left to fire
    His angry darts.
First one and then another smarts,
Until no longer they can stand
The stings he gives on ev'ry hand.

They gather round him and complain.
" Messieurs," said he, " your talk is vain ;
It is my nature so to do,
And I can't change it to please *you.*"
The leader then exclaim'd—" My friend,
If such bad manners you can't mend ;
If you cannot your quills suppress,
At least draw over them some dress ;
Or, failing this, then let me say,
From decent people stay away."

THE WHITE ELEPHANT.

Far in a certain eastern land
The people in great rev'rence stand
In presence of the elephant.
He's lodg'd in style most elegant
(That is, if so the brute be white),
And for him men fierce battles fight:
    For prize so rare
    States go to war;
He's always serv'd on golden plate;
And so divine is his estate
That when folks meet him walking forth,
They bow before him to the earth.

One of these people's pets one day
(A sound clear thinker by the way)
To his conductor said:—" I pray
Why are such honors shown to me?
For I am but a beast, you see."
" Ah! you're too humble," said his guide:
    "We know what's due
    To one like you;
And all our India knows beside,
That when our heroes come to die,
Their souls into your body fly,
And there for some time must endure.
    Priests tell us so,
    And hence we know,
    The thing is sure."

"What! do you think us heroes then?"
"Yes; so believe our best of men."
"And should we, if it were not so,
     Be free to go
And wander through the wide domain
Of our own native woods again?"
"Oh yes, my Lord."—"Then let me go;
For you're deceiv'd, as I can show:—
Our race is proud, yet still caressing;
Gentle, though great power possessing;
We never hurt, as you may see,
Nor injure those less strong than we:
Our hearts can love, yet, from lust free,
Observe the laws of chastity;
And ne'er do we our honors earn
By loss of virtue in return.
Since this is so, how can you then,
Think we possess the souls of men?"

FABLE XL.

THE GUILTY DOG.

At length the awful news was spread—
Towser had kill'd the pet lamb dead!
Who could believe the tidings true,
That Towser such a deed would do?
The dread of wolves, the shepherd's friend—
How could he come to such an end?

And not alone a lamb he'd kill'd,
But her own mother's blood had spill'd!
    Nor was this the worst of it,
      For e'en the shepherd he had bit!
      If this be true,
Then what's the world a-coming to?

'Twas thus beside a brooklet's course,
Two sheep engaged in sad discourse.
It was an undisputed fact,
He had been captured in the act.
Towser himself confess'd his crime,
And would be punish'd in short time.
The shepherds had resolv'd that he
A warning to all dogs should be.

With triple murder being charg'd,
The case went through the court with speed,
Upon the crime the judge enlarged—
The witnesses were all agreed,
And he was sentenced to be shot
Upon the very self-same spot
    Where he had done the deed.
The whole farm then turn'd out to see
    The execution done.
The lambs beseeched for clemency;
    The farmer granted none.
He made them take their place assign'd;
The dogs took their's near by, resign'd,
Humbled and lorn, with drooping ears;
The cheeks of some were bath'd in tears.

All mourn'd for their friend Towser's fate,
And all in fun'ral silence sate,
 Or sobbing cried aloud.
At length between two shepherds bound,
Towser was led upon the ground,
 And thus address'd the crowd:

"Oh, you whom I no longer dare
To call my friends as formerly,
Of my example all beware,
And take this warning word from me.
A virtuous course of fifteen years
Is now to close in blood and tears.

"My crimes are these :—at early day
As I near by a forest lay,
Guarding the flock, a wolf sprang out,
And bore a bleeding lamb away.
We fought—I put him to the rout.
So far so good. But when I saw
The mangled lambkin near me lie,
And felt the tempting morsel draw,
I could not help one taste to try.
 The sight and smell of blood
Had made me ravenous for food.
'Tis true I hesitated long,
But yet my appetite was strong;
And so I yielded, and at last,
Of the slain lamb made a repast ;
 Such was the source of all my woe.
The mother sheep I fear'd might go

And tell the shepherd what I'd done,
And say that I had kill'd her son.
So therefore without more ado
To silence her, I kill'd her too.
    My head was turn'd ;
    With rage I burn'd ;
And what I did I hardly knew;
I even at my master flew.
Until at last I am brought here,
To terminate my sad career.
From this career you may take heed,
Lest your small faults to great ones lead.
The slightest wrong, however small,
May lead the wisest to his fall.
Of all false steps beware of this—
The first one towards a precipice."

FABLE XLI.

THE SAGE ADVICE.

A flying-fish, tired of her lot,
Unto her mother thus complain'd :—
"You may be pleas'd, but I am not,

To live forever thus constrain'd.
   I cannot leap into the air,
   But what the eagle's waiting there.
And if I dive into the sea,
The dolphin there is after me."
The dame replied in accents mild,
" I've found in this strange world, my child,
   And now must let you know,
For medium folks as you and I,
We should not ever soar too high,
   Nor ever dive too low."

FABLE XLII.
THE DOG AND CAT.

'Tis of a dog the story's told,
How, being by his master sold,
At his new home he would not stay,
But broke his chain and ran away.
Returning to his old abode,
How great was his surprise to find
That no one there a welcome show'd,

Or friendliness of any kind!
He found no greeting as before,
 But with rebuffs,
 And kicks and cuffs,
Was driven from the door.
Grimalkin sat with wond'ring eyes
As she beheld her friend's surprise,
And ventur'd this remark to make:
"That you and I are lov'd, 'tis true;
But what a fool, indeed, are you,
To think we're priz'd for *our* sake!"

FABLE XLIII.

THE CANARY AND THE CROW.

Together were two cages hung,
    For music and for show;
In one a fine canary sung,
    In t'other screech'd a crow.
One charm'd the household with his song,
The other vex'd it with his cries;
Forever cawing all day long,
He call'd for bread, and cakes, and pies.

And people fed him to his fill,
As the best way to keep him still.
Loud rang the sweet canary's strain,
He ask'd for naught, and sung in vain.
For none supplied his pressing needs,
Or gave him water, or his seeds.

Those most delighted by his chants,
Were quite oblivious of his wants.
They liked him well enough, 'twas true,
But never gave him what was due.
At last one day they found him dead,
Merely for want of being fed.
"Alas!" folks cried, "how can we spare
A songster so beyond compare!
How could he die?—a bird so rare!"

But while they thus express surprise,
The crow keeps up his stunning cries,
And still is fed on cakes and pies.

FABLE XLIV.

THE MONKEY WITH A MAGIC LANTERN.

All gentlemen who verses write,
In style magnificent and grand,
But who can ne'er a line indite,
Which common folks may understand,
Please listen to the tale I tell.

And on its meaning ponder well.
A man whose business 'twas to show
   A magic lantern round,
Had a fine monkey, hight Jacqueau,
The nicest trickster ever found.
He could dance, and leap, and spring;
Was great at tight-rope balancing;
A thousand tricks this Jacqueau knew,
Which custom to his master drew.

One day his master went away,
To celebrate some holiday,
And left him at the inn to stay.
There entered then this monkey's head,
The strangest fancy ever bred:
For what does he but straightway go,
    To cats and dogs,
    To hens and hogs,
    To geese and ducks,
    And turkey-cocks,
To come and see the magic show.

"Walk in, Messieurs; I nothing ask;
Believe me, 'tis a pleasing task!"

They take their seats; the lantern's brought;
He makes a speech most highly wrought,
Which—as we say in modern lore—
Was welcom'd with a perfect roar.
Encouraged by the warm applause,
The window shutters then he draws,
Into the lantern puts a screen

As he had oft his master seen—
" Here you may see," said he, " the sun,
His pristine glory just begun ;
And presently the moon you'll see,
And the first pair's felicity,
Adam and Eve, and all our race—
Behold what beauty ! and what grace !
    Was ever anything so fine ?
And here you'll see a sight divine."

But how could they behold the sight,
Where all was close and dark as night ?
However much their eyes they strain,
And strive to see, they strive in vain.
" My faith ! " th' impatient cat exclaim'd,
" Of all the wonders he has nam'd—
Of all the sights he's dwelt upon,
I have not seen a single one."
" Neither have I," the dog replied ;
" I've not a single thing descried."
The turkey something saw, he thought,
But could not tell exactly what.
Yet little this concern'd Jacqueau,
Who rattled on like Cicero.
His style was good and masterly ;
His language choice, and diction free ;
But *one* thing he'd forgotten quite—
Although he work'd his lantern right,
He had not put therein a light !

FABLE XLV.

THREE FORTUNE-SEEKERS.

An ermine, beaver, and young boar,
Who had no fortune 'neath the sun,
But who had hopes of getting one.
Set out the country to explore.
At last, their many trials o'er.
They reach'd a most delightful land,

Where beauties shone on ev'ry hand,
In wealth of meadows, orchards, woods,
And all the treasures of the floods.
Our pilgrims seeing scenes so fair,
Were in a perfect ecstasy,
As Æneas and his Trojans were,
With their first view of Italy.
But all this happy land, alas!
Lay circled by a black morass.
Where frightful lizards, snakes, and toads
Were wont to make their foul abodes.
Brought to a stop, they take a view,
And ponder what they're next to do.
The ermine trying with her paw,
Decides at once that she'll withdraw.
" My friends," said she, " take my advice,
This land is not so very nice.
To reach it we must cross the slough,
And that my coat would ruin so,
     That I should die.
Some other country let us try."
" Have patience, dear," the beaver said :
" These things require a little head.
We need not always get a stain,
In coming at the point we'd gain.
As I'm a mason, I can throw,
In fifteen days o'er this foul slough
A bridge by which we can pass o'er,
And harmless reach the farther shore."
" In fifteen days!" exclaim'd the boar :

" The thing much sooner can be done ;
I'll show you how in less than one."
Then in he leaps into the slime,
Amidst the lizards, toads, and snakes ;
Most lustily his way he makes,
And flounders over in short time.
Arriv'd upon the other side,
He shook the mud off from his hide,
And then with pompous, proud display,
Back to his friends this scorn he hurl'd :—
" If you would prosper in this world,
You must, as I've done, push your way."

FABLE XLVI.

THE PERSECUTED POODLE.

A shaggy poodle being shorn
So as to have a lion's mane,
Could hardly longer well be borne,
He so conceited was and vain;
For vanity will sure deceive

All who her flattery receive.
We on this head a story know.
It came to pass, not long ago,
That after long and bloody strife,
Where many a lion lost his life,
The elephant the victor was,
Who thereupon decreed these laws :—
That brawls and blood-shed to prevent,
All into exile must be sent
Who civil war and strife foment ;
And never more should lions come
Within his realms to make their home.
The lions, overcome, subdu'd,
And by their enemies pursu'd,
Were hunted down on ev'ry hand,
And forc'd to fly and leave the land.
Their fate admitted no relief :
But still they made the best of it.
They kept their courage with their grief,
And learn'd in patience to submit.
But with our poodle 'twas not so :
The dread decree fill'd him with woe.
" Oh, am I then," he moaning cried,
" No longer suffer'd here to dwell ?
Must I in other lands reside,
Far from the scenes I've lov'd so well ?
     And in my old age too !
Oh barb'rous king to drive me forth
From this dear spot that gave me birth,
     Which I no more shall view !

I go unaided and in gloom,
In foreign lands to seek a tomb:
And even that may be denied!
And all to please this tyrant's pride,
Who only thus is satisfied!"
A spaniel heard the pug complain,
And touch'd at heart with so much pain,
Ask'd why he felt obliged to fly.
" *Why?* " said the pug, " do you ask *why!*
Just look and see that hard decree,
How cruel and severe on me!"

  The spaniel cried :—
" That law with *lions* has to do ;
But what concern is that to *you!* "

  The pug replied :—
" Why, am not *I* a lion too!"

FABLE XLVII.

THE DOVE AND THE MAGPIE.

Once on a time a dove had built
Her nest near where a magpie dwelt.
It must be own'd the neighborhood
Could not be reckon'd very good.
But that is neither here nor there ;
We simply state things as they were.
    In the dwelling of the dove,

Ev'rything was peace and love,
While in t'other all was strife—
Husband fighting with the wife,
Broken eggs and wretched life.
Twas one day after being beat,
The magpie sought the dove's retreat,
Where she chatter'd, scolded, cried
Told all she knew and more beside,
And with her clamor fill'd the house
About the failings of her spouse.
" He is exacting, hard, and proud,"
She shriek'd aloud,
" And passionate and jealous too ;
And yet he goes
To see the crows,
As I can well attest to you."
And in her anger she gave vent
To many things of like intent.
" But *you*," the gentle dove replied,
" Have you no faults on *your* side ? "
" I *have*," the pie resum'd, " 'tis true ;
And I may say, between us two,
In my behavior I've been light,
And sometimes shown a deal of spite.
I've often, too, play'd the coquette,
Merely to see him writhe and fret."
(Pies hardly would this fault admit
If they thought doves would credit it.)
" But what of that ? I'd like to know,
Don't other birds do even so ? "

" Oh no, indeed," the dove rejoined ;
" You'll never peace in that way find.
If thus you irritate your mate,
You give him cause for all his hate."
"*I* give him cause !" the pie exclaim'd,
With anger at the dove inflam'd,
"That's very bright, upon my word !
Such impudence who ever heard ?
When I come here for sympathy,
You set about abusing me !
Keep your advice at home, say I,
And so, impertinence, good bye !"
Quite too indignant to say more,
She flung impatient from the door,
Enraged to find herself oppos'd.
By her own faults which she'd disclos'd.

FABLE XLVIII.

THE SQUIRREL, THE DOG, AND THE FOX.

A dog and squirrel hand in hand,
Where one time trav'ling through the land,
When they were caught as night came down,
In a large forest far from town.
No friendly inn was there t'afford

Its hospitable bed and board.
So in an old and hollow tree,
    The dog for shelter search'd,
While his good friend, the squirrel, he
    Among the branches perch'd.
Towards midnight, at that solemn hour
When to their crimes sly murd'rers creep,
When somnolence asserts its power,
And our two friends were sunk in sleep,
Lo! an old fox athirst for blood,
Came prowling through the silent wood.
He saw the squirrel on a limb,
    And thus accosted him :—
"My friend, I pray you pardon me,
I would not so intrusive be
As to disturb your sweet repose,
But that I'm dying to disclose
My true heart-felt felicity
    To find that you and I
In blood relationship are nigh:
We're cousins of the first degree !
For your good mother, I've heard said,
Was sister to my worthy sire,
Who bade me, on his dying bed,
For you, his nephew, to inquire,
And give you half the legacy
    He left for me.
So haste, my friend, come down I pray,
And have your portion right away.
I burn to meet you face to face,

More fully to explain the case.
If I, like you, could climb a tree,
Indeed, you well may credit me,
I had been with you long ere this,
To show how great my pleasure is."
Now squirrels though not bred in schools.
Are not by any means all fools;
And ours was shrewd enough to see
Quite through the fox's knavery.
So he replied in tones most kind :—
" I am delighted, friend, to find
That we so near related are.
Your happiness I fully share ;
And I shall hurry to descend.
But ere I come I have a friend
That I would introduce to you.
He is a near relation too :
One who is all in all to me,
Whom you'll be glad, perhaps, to see ;
He's sleeping in that hole below ;
Knock at the door and call him out:
He'll warmly welcome you, I know,
On learning what you've come about."
Old Reynard hurries to the door,
Hoping to get one squirrel more ;
But on the instant that he knocks,
The dog, awak'd from slumbers sound,
Springs out, and at a single bound,
Upon the spot kills Mister Fox.

The offices of a true friend

May not alone our life defend :
No greater blessing can there be,
Than solace from his sympathy.

———————

KING ALPHONSO.

A certain king who held his reign
Where Tagus mingles with the main,
Alphonso called, surnam'd The Wise—
(Not so surnam'd because discreet,
But just because he thought it meet
    To scan the skies)—
Knew much of all phenomena,
And was a great astronomer.
More of the heavens he came to know,
Than of his kingdom here below :
For when to council call'd, he'd soon
Run off to view the sun or moon.
At length one day when going to
His telescope to take a view,
The gentry round him he address'd :—
"Messieurs! I am at last possess'd
Of instruments, by which, to-night,
I hope to see the wond'rous sight
Of men within our satellite !"
"No doubt you will," a courtier cried,
"And many other things beside."
Meantime a poor street-beggar bow'd,
And ask'd for pennies from the crowd.

The king could neither hear nor see
The man's appeal for charity ;
But all absorb'd pursu'd his way,
Unheeding what the man might say.
Yet still the beggar humbly pray'd ;
Beseeching held his hand for aid,
And much the king did importune.
But still the king with thoughts on high,
Made ever still this same reply :—
" I shall see men within the moon."
At last the poor man in distress,
Seiz'd on the monarch's royal dress,
    And gravely said :—
" You'll find men *here*, men who need bread :
You need not look for them up there ;
They're here, around you, ev'rywhere.
This realm God gave you for a boon,
Not one up yonder in the moon."

FABLE L.

DEATH'S CHOICE OF PRIME MINISTER.

Once on a time there was a king
Who wish'd his state more flourishing.
In hell he rear'd his awful throne,
(As King of Terrors he is known)
And, as the case did much import,
He call'd together his whole court.
The question was what plague should be
The chief aid to his majesty.
First, from the lowest hell there came

Three spirits of most dreadful fame,
  FEVER, GOUT, and WAR.
Death gave them welcome; for, of all
The ills that plague our earthly ball,
  These most dreaded are.
Then PEST steps forward—all agree
That he too, has great potency.
Then comes a DOCTOR, at whose name
'Twas evident he had a claim,
Which caused e'en Death himself to doubt
How his selection must turn out.
But when the VICES all advance,
Death could no longer hesitate
Which most his service would enhance,
Or which was his true candidate:
Vice of all vice—INTEMPERANCE—
He chose prime minister of state.

FABLE LI.

THE JOURNEY.

To set out ere the dawn of day,
Groping in darkness for the way,
Caring for naught, nor making quest
If going North, South, East, or West;—
From fall to fall to stumble on
Till near one-third the course be run:
Then, as the dark clouds gather round,
To enter on unstable ground,
Yet pushing onwards, though quite lost,
'Midst thick'ning doubts, and tempest tost,

With no sure aim, no end in view,
And seldom knowing what to do ;—
Driven, forc'd on, and in great stress,
Seeking some spot, some safe recess,
Where to arrive all out of breath,
    And there to creep
    To the last sleep—
Such then is BIRTH, and LIFE, and DEATH;
This is the way we journey on :—
    God's will be done !

CLOSING LINES.

    "Tis done: the lyre is mute ;
My labors here must have an end ;
Though still the Muse might wrongs impute,
That should perchance our manners mend,
(If she but had an abler friend).

But no ; her work would prove in vain ;
For the world's folly, int'rest, pride,
Will e'er bring trouble in their train,
However much they be decried.
'Tis vain that philosophic sects
May censure man for his defects ;
They waste their wisdom and their rhymes.
Let the world wag ! Go with the times !

Or live retir'd, content and free,
In some deep-hid obscurity.
There, what could fail us that might bless

Our lives with perfect happiness?
Save gentle peace, a tranquil lot;
Our only wish to be forgot;
Our sole endeavor how to shun
The ills by which we're prey'd upon;
With wealth enough with friends to share,
But not to waken envy there.

THE END

www.ingramcontent.com/pod-product-compliance
Lightning Source LLC
Chambersburg PA
CBHW022139020726
47496CB00008B/2462